THIS ZOO IS NOT FOR YOU

For Corra and Cairn –
this zoo is for you

First published 2017 by Nosy Crow Ltd
The Crow's Nest, 14 Baden Place, Crosby Row
London SE1 1YW
www.nosycrow.com

This edition published 2018
ISBN 978 1 78800 252 3

Nosy Crow and associated logos are trademarks and/or
registered trademarks of Nosy Crow Ltd.
Text and illustrations copyright © Ross Collins 2017
The right of Ross Collins to be identified as the author
and illustrator of this work has been asserted.

A CIP catalogue record for this book
is available from the British Library.
Printed in China
Papers used by Nosy Crow are made from
wood grown in sustainable forests.

10 9 8 7 6 5 4 3 2 1

nosy crow

ROSS COLLINS

THIS ZOO IS NOT FOR YOU

Hello, come in.

How do you do?

Have you come

for the interview?

A platypus!

That's strange and new!

You're meeting Panda first –

go through.

I'm special, rare
and **famous** too.

To get me here
was **quite** a coup.
But you don't even
eat **bamboo**!

I think, this zoo
is **not** for you.

We're elegant and graceful too.
We really do **enhance** the view.

But you look like
a **worn-out shoe.**

And so this zoo
is **not** for you.

We're **very** good at throwing poo.
Young Jeffrey here can play **kazoo**.

Is there a **trick** that you can do?
If not, this zoo
is **not** for you.

We are a multicoloured crew.
I'm **green**, then **red**,
then **pink**, or **blue**.

You're brownish-grey
– but just **one** hue.

It's clear this zoo
is **not** for you.

I'm powerful
and **huge**, it's true.

You are short
and quite weird too.

You've simply **failed**
this interview.

You see, this zoo
is **not** for you.

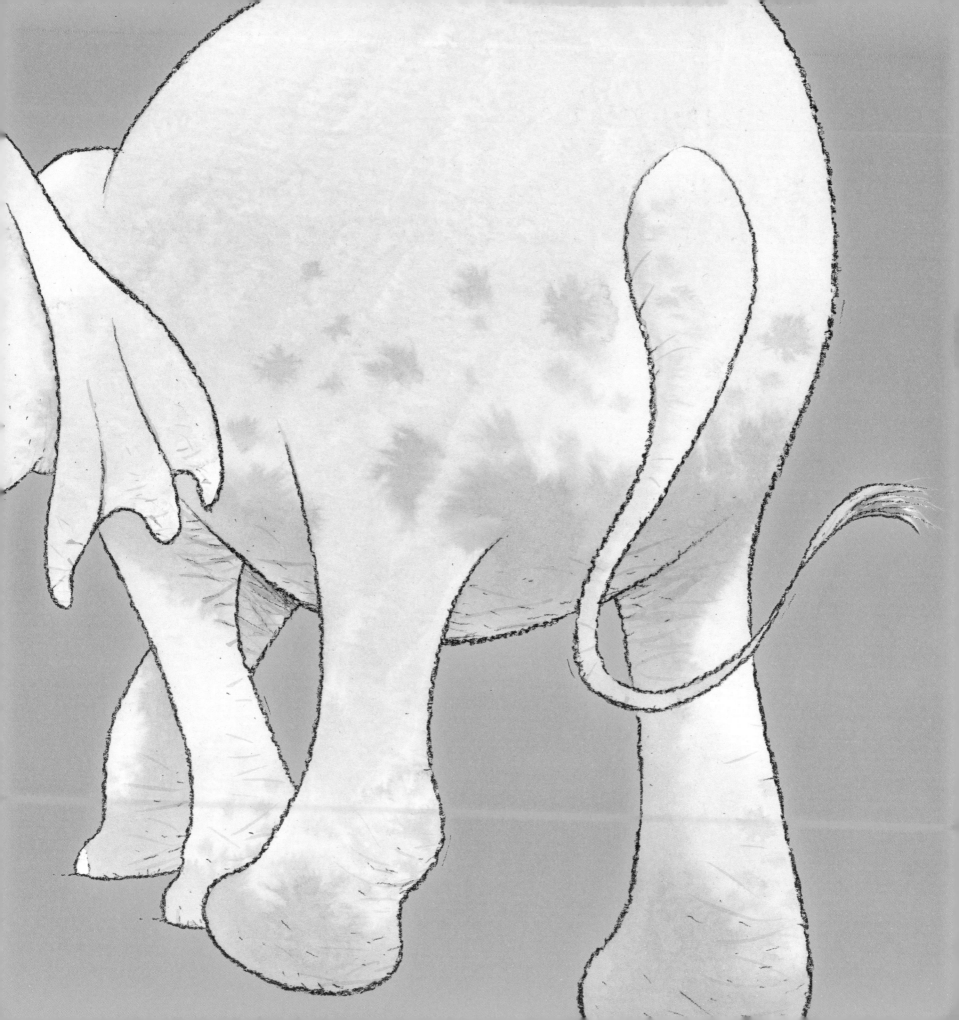

How did you find the interview?
I think I was **unkind**. Were you?

Perhaps he **could** have
joined our zoo.

But now he's gone.
What **shall** we do?

We **must** apologise to you –
you didn't **want** to
join our zoo.
We got it **wrong** –
that much is true.

We found your
invitation too!

We'd **love** to be
good friends . . .

. . . would you?

Relax,

guys . . .

This **platybus** is
for **all** of us!